Talk-Along —

HELP
JUMBO
ESCAPE

by Dick Punnett
illustrated by
Tom Dunnington

THE
CHILD'S
WORLD

ELGIN, ILLINOIS 60120

Distributed by Childrens Press, 1224 West Van Buren Street, Chicago, Illinois 60607

Library of Congress Cataloging in Publication Data

Punnett, Richard Douglas.
  Talk along—help Jumbo escape.

  (A Talk-along book)
  Summary: The reader helps a lost elephant
find his mother by supplying the missing word
which rhymes with the preceding line.
  [1. Stories in rhyme. 2. Elephants—
Fiction] I. Dunnington, Tom, ill. II. Title.
III. Title: Help Jumbo escape. IV. Series.
PZ8.3.P97He   [E]   81-21667
ISBN 0 89565-214-5   AACR2

To my wife, YVONNE,
the best "talk-along" partner a man ever had!

I want you to know before we start,
Our story has a speaking part.
When you see the dots . . .
        try guessing the word.
That is the time for YOU to be heard.

Poor Little Jumbo—he's lost his mother.
And every trail looks just like the other.
He needs your help. It's time to talk.
Tell Little Jumbo to take a . . .

walk

He didn't get far, as you can see.
A snake is hiding in a tree.
Jumbo is scared! His mind is blank.
Quick, get him loose! Tell him to . . .

yank

He obeyed your command, but who is that beast
Crouched in the grass—waiting to feast?
A tiger! He's hungry! Will Jumbo survive?
Look at that water! Tell him to . . .

dive

You saved little Jumbo and the tiger's upset.
He won't follow Jumbo 'cause he hates to get wet!

Jumbo is sinking!
Things look very grim.
Our story is over,
Unless you say . . .

swim

He swam for his life, but he sees a new trap.
Something behind him is ready to snap!
The shore is so far—let's get him up high.
There's only one way. Tell Jumbo to . . .

fly

Not a second too soon, Jumbo heard you shout.
And he blasted off—on a water spout!
That branch up above is the right one to nab,
So speak up at once, and tell him to . . .

grab

He's safe in a tree, at least for a while,
But waiting below is that crocodile.
To hang by the nose is a difficult thing.
Before he lets go, you must tell him to . . .

swing

He swung through the air and shattered a nest!
Down dives a hawk, looking distressed.
A hawk in a rage is really no fun;
Tell Little Jumbo to get up and . . .

run

The trail 'round the mountain is not very wide,
And the mean old bear will not step aside.
If they crash, they will fall with a mighty flop.
Warn Little Jumbo to come to a . . .

stop

Jumbo obeyed, but he's still filled with dread
'Cause the hawk is behind—and the bear is ahead!
Either will eat him; he's tender and plump.

Below is a tree,
So tell him to . . .

23

jump

Now here's something else to add to his woes.
Some monkeys have started to tickle his toes.
He *can* call for help if only he'd try.
Quickly and loudly, tell him to . . .

cry

Jumbo cried and cried; then he heard something sweet—
A faraway rumble of thundering feet.

Mother is coming! She has to find out
Which tree he is in, so tell him to . . .

shout

At last he is safe! Now aren't you proud?
You saved Little Jumbo—by talking out loud.
Since Mother is holding our elephant friend,
Our story is over, and this is the . . .

end

About the Author:

Dick Punnett lives on what he calls a "smoky little Florida river." His home on the Tomoka houses a rare, old carousel horse which sometimes gives rides to visiting children. Mr. Punnett grew up in Penfield, New York. He studied art at Principia College in Elsah, Illinois. And after further studies at the Art Center School and Chouinard Art Institute in Los Angeles, he became a writer-cartoonist for a Hollywood animation studio.

About the Artist:

Tom Dunnington hails from the Midwest, having lived in Minnesota, Iowa, Illinois, and Indiana. He attended the John Herron Institute of Art in Indianapolis and the American Academy of Art and the Chicago Art Institute in Chicago. He has been an art instructor and illustrator for many years. In addition to illustrating books, Mr. Dunnington is working on a series of paintings of endangered birds (produced as limited edition prints). His current residence is in Oak Park, Illinois, where he works as a free-lance illustrator and is active in church and community youth work.